Burnt Rainbows

By C. J. Henning

Other titles found on amazon.com, Booksamillion, and Barnes and Noble. Search C J Henning and the following titles will appear:

FANTASY

Saga of Everstream: Tiathan Eiula and the War of the Seven Fortresses Vol. 1&2

Whirlwind Sage and the Arbushi Wars

Nursery Rhyme and Fairy Tale Mysteries

More Mysteries of Fairy Tales and Nursery Rhymes

John Taddleboch and the Weegie Worts

John Taddleboch Meets Twiggle

Tittle Tattle Tales

DRAMA

The Plays Vol. 1&2

COMMENTARIES

Common Sense or Who's That Sitting In My Pew?

Common Sense, Too or Are You Still Sitting In My Pew?

I Will Not Apologize For Christ

Death And Dying, An Uplifting Social Commentary

FICTION

Wormwood

On The Morning Of the First Day

Preface

Don't go chasing waterfalls or staring at rainbows. If you are not in love, they are only burnt effigies of hope.

Terror At Night

I walked the same path every night for twenty years with never of thought I was in danger. Tonight the rustling of leaves and a hot breath of wind changed all that. It was October and the temperature was in the forties.

I was halfway between home and my job so I continued on looking over my shoulder. I didn't recognize if what I heard was footsteps or the pounding of my heart. Searching the side brush, I saw nothing that would give me pause.

A young couple walked towards me in the other direction holding hands and kissing. They surely would have heard what I heard, but they only had eyes for each other. As they passed me, she giggled and winked at me.

I relaxed a little as they seemed to be safely away. A few steps further I heard a slight gasp of surprise. I turned to find they had vanished from the street. There was nowhere to go for another block.

The urge to run away was strong, yet I had to know where they went. I started back to where I last saw them. I found her purse and a set of keys on the ground.

I called out though I didn't know their names. There was no answer except I felt a hot breeze brush past my face. I was sure something was there as I froze solidly in place.

A shadow from the thick brush moved from side to side. I relaxed when I saw the young girl smiling at me as she winked. The problem was that her head was held by the tentacles of some huge creature.

All I wanted to do was run, but where? The woman's head disappeared from sight as the head of some monstrous creature looked straight at me. Its eyes bulged as if it wanted to play.

When I ran left, it followed me laying its tentacles in my way. Terrified I sought escape to my right. I found myself knocked down by a slimy appendage on the back of my neck.

I woke up in the morning with police surrounding me. Others were in the brush shaking their heads in dismay. On the ground was the young woman's head. They asked me what happened which my explanation would immediately have me taken away.

I don't walk the same path every night now and have told no one what I saw. No matter where I go I have the feeling of dread though every shadow I encounter I see image of a crusty eye.

Birds of Prey

It's that time of year where the birds migrate around our cabin. They usually sing and chirp for a week and then continue on their way. For some reason they have stayed a second week and landed on the ground watching our cabin.

It became unnerving when some of them landed on our windowsill staring in on us while we ate. I thought it would be nice to go outside to see why they stayed so long.

There were blackbirds, robins and crows seemingly staring down at me when I went outside. I knew not to feed them because I wanted them to go away on their journey.

As I looked around, I didn't see the crow flying straight at me. I ducked at the last minute before a robin followed after it. Soon a few others chased me back inside. I heard a thump, thump on the door. I checked to find two blackbirds had slammed into my door and broken their necks.

My wife, Susan, hurriedly ran to the bedroom and brought out two hunting rifles. She told me she remembered Hitchcock's movie and wasn't going to take any chances. Considering what just happened, I agreed with her.

We thought of running to the car and leaving, but it was covered with crows. I noticed the front and rear windows were smashed with the entrails of birds sticking out of the cracks.

As the sun went down, we turned on the lights only to hear a sizzling sound knocking out the electricity. In the dim light a few birds had sacrificed themselves to put us in the dark. Susan was noticeably shivering worried what they were going to do next.

Headlights shone into the cabin as a truck with two rangers drove into the driveway. Within seconds loud screeching and the sound of loud crashing pierced the darkness. Screams of pain and agony came close to our front door before silence.

Something was banging on our front window which we had replaced with hurricane glass. A number of birds flew head on without success to break through. All through the night, a barrage of banging and thumping kept us up.

By morning the assault stopped and we drifted off to sleep from sheer exhaustion. I awoke first seeing the bloody mess on the windows. However, there was an eerie quiet that led me to look outside.

There were hundreds of birds lying dead on the ground as well as the torn bodies of the two rangers. Susan looked out the back, but the birds had left.

We quickly packed and left the cabin. When we reached town, we saw more dead birds and the town deserted. We continued down the road and as we reached the edge, I saw in my rear view mirror the gathering of crows following us.

Mattapoisett

My wife Barbara and I finally, finally were able to have a quiet vacation for a month. We decided to rent a cottage at Mattapoisett, Massachusetts. The cottage was only three hundred feet from the beach with only a few other residents as neighbors.

Our first night gave us a spectacular view of a sunset with the waves gently washing across the sand. We finished unpacking and went to a local restaurant that served fresh Swordfish. It seemed as though everything would be perfect.

The next morning, as usual for us, we got up to see the sunrise. As we walked down toward the beach we heard voices and laughter. Just as we reached the path to the beach we saw four older ladies sitting facing the ocean.

We introduced ourselves finding out the older woman was Hannah, then Winnie. Mary and Betty. They stared at us for a few moments before talking to each other.

"No politics today, girls." Hannah appeared to be their leader.

"How about gossip?" Mary licked her lips bursting with some juicy tidbit to tell everyone.

"Maybe we should leave." Barbara nudged me away.

"No, stay!" Betty fiercely insisted that we don't leave.

"How long have you ladies lived here?" I asked to change the subject.

"It's seems forever." Winnie looked forlornly out over the ocean.

"We are here most mornings when people like you come to stay." Hannah's eyes glistened in the morning haze.

"Sort of a greeting group." Barbara thought they were cute.

As we talked I felt the first lap of water caress my feet. I didn't think we were that close to the water. The little old ladies continued to smile at us as we shared talk of our families.

I noticed that the waves were now washing

against their chairs. There was an odd look to each of their feet as the water covered their toes. Before long Barbara and I were waist deep in the water not knowing how we got to that point. Hannah and her crew seemed to float off their chairs.

Barbara panicked when she saw the first large fin appear behind Winnie. I followed her out of the water while looking back the four women who now had scaly skin and beginning to sing a soothing melodic tune.

The music beckoned us back into the water. We held our ears before running from the beach. When we were safely far enough away, we looked back to see four large fish tails diving into the waves.

No Exit

I walked through this cemetery for the past two years listening to the birds and watching squirrels chase each other up and down trees. There were no clouds today making it a perfect beginning of my day

After a couple of hours I grew tired probably because being seventy years old, I wasn't used to being on my feet so long. I sat down for a moment under an old oak tree and closed my eyes.

I awoke noticing it was getting late in the afternoon. I got up and started toward the entrance t the cemetery. I could see the metal frame in the distance and started out thinking of chili I would heat up for a meal

I looked down at the ground for a moment and then raised my head. I found myself in the same spot where I started. Funny thing, I thought, but I saw the entrance of the cemetery ahead of me and walked towards it again.

It was getting darker so I hurried my steps to be on my way home. I rubbed my eyes to clear the moisture of tears that seemed to run down my cheek. I blinked a couple of times before finding I was in the same spot where I started.

The shadows from the trees and tombstones seemed to reach out as the sun set. The branches twisted into gnarled hands trying to grab my legs and arms. I started to run only to find I was going in circles.

My heart raced in fear finding it hard to breathe. I stumbled over rocks and roots ignoring the pain of hitting the ground. It was difficult to get up as an oppressive need to sleep overwhelmed me.

I forced myself up and looked for a path to escape. It was then I saw someone sitting against a tree to my right. I was able to relax a little knowing I wasn't alone.

As I came closer, there was something familiar about this man. I leaned over to look closer finding he looked like me. I reached over to try and wake him. Immediately, I found myself sitting under the old oak.

The darkness had gone as I stood up. I wondered if I just had a bad dream except the scuff marks on my pants where I tripped over the rocks and limbs.

I saw the metal frame of the cemetery sign and cautiously walked towards it. This time I was able to leave the cemetery. I gave a sigh of relief though I vowed never to go in there again. I would be there soon enough.

Haunted Parish

We paid nine dollars each to visit what was called a haunted parish in a small town of Harrod, Pennsylvania. It was off the interstate advertised on a crumpled sign off exit 123. Judy and I thought it might be interesting to take a look. How scary could it be?

We were met by three priests with silly smiles on their face. They told us we were the first visitors to come by that morning. The haunted parish was just behind them looking exactly as the broken building that was advertised.

"Do you get many visitors?" Judy asked looking skeptical that they could afford to keep the place open. She thought maintenance had to be cheap.

"Enough." One of the priests spoke with hollowness in his voice.

The other two nodded in agreement. We were shown to the front door and into a great hall. We heard singing coming from the loft overlooking the room.

There was a choir singing, but by the trick of the light from the stained glass windows, they were ghostly images. I thought the special effects were worth the visit.

All three priests walked with us as we ventured in and out of various rooms. We were told there were chambers beneath the parish showing various means of torture that those who were disbelievers were subjected to all sorts of pain.

Judy was not in favor of seeing any of it. I was tempted, but opted to see the clergy room and the library. Cobwebs greeted us in the library where books seemed never to be read. Our guides never spoke another word, but smiled as I pointed out an old Bible opened to Revelation.

An image of a choir member in a white robe flitted just outside my peripheral vision. When I turned for a better look, the image was gone. Judy felt a chill and wanted to leave.

We wanted to leave and yet had the urge to stay. We thanked our hosts who almost reached out to hold us back. Tears slipped down their cheeks as we went back to our car. Looking back, we saw that they were gone.

A police car drove into the parking lot and an officer stepped out. He asked us what we were doing there. I told him we were just inside with three priests who guided us through the church.

The officer was confused. He told us that the church had been closed for twenty years after three priests were killed when part of the roof collapsed on them.

The officer told us no one had been in there for a long time and it was dangerous to go inside. Now we were confused as we left the parking lot. Who were the three priests we met? Were they ghosts? Impersonators?

Don't Call Me

When the phone rang I thought it was my wife, Linda. I said "Hello?" yet no one answered. I thought it was a telemarketing glitch and hung up.

The phone rang again and this time a harsh deep voice said "Don't call me." He then hung up before I could say it was he who called me. A third time the phone rang it was Linda saying she tried to call earlier but the line was busy.

Linda told me she was working late and not

to worry. A few minutes later the phone rang again.

"I said not to call me!" the same angry voice bellowed over the phone.

"I didn't call y..." He had hung up.

The rest of the night was quiet, but I wondered what was going on. Linda came home and told me she thought she was being followed. We passed it off as nothing. Linda did tell me she would be working late the next day.

After I had my dinner that night, I leaned back to read the newspapers. The phone rang with the same harsh voice on the other end.

"Don't call me!" The voice insisted. "You'll regret it if you do. I know where your wife works."

"How...?" He slammed the phone down.

I called the police, but not knowing who or

where the calls came from, they could do nothing. I thought of meeting Linda at work, but instead called her to be careful.

I don't know how I got this guy mad at us, but I kept my shotgun handy and placed two hunting knives in places I could easily get to. I was on edge the rest of the night.

I must have fallen asleep on the couch when the phone rang. This time it was Linda whose voice was shaking.

"Help me!" Linda was in a panic.

"Where are you?" I asked hearing someone else in the background.

"I told you not to call me!" The angry voice pulled Linda from the phone.

"I never called you!" I yelled into the phone. "I don't know why you are doing this!"

"Because." Was all he said before hanging up.

Linda's body was found a mile from our home. She had been shot and a note was found pinned to her coat which read "Call me"

Danse Macabre

I heard music coming from my back woods soon after a burning effigy was placed on my lawn. I have no idea why I was singled out, but there was no explanation that came from my neighbors or the police.

I stepped down from my church as pastor a few weeks ago. Maybe this was a message of being unwanted in the community. I was told it might have been my sermons that undid me. I did not agree with the many social issues that went against scripture.

I was sent threatening letters seeking my death or, at the very least, expulsion from the town. I heard rumors that my conservative interpretation of the Bible was not welcome with most of my congregation.

Many told me my words hurt the feelings of those who were blatantly standing against God with their lifestyles. I was told certain passages would not allow individuals to enjoy life to the fullest. That my views were archaic where I relied on the strict interpretation of scripture.

Most of my parish were insulted and angry until I had no support. Maybe it was cowardice, but I resigned when the death threats came too close to home. The chanting in the woods chilled me up and down my spine.

Finally, on the third night, of music and torches in my woods, I ventured out into the darkness. About a hundred feet from my back yard I found a large gathering standing in a circle.

The music of guitars, drums and flutes cascaded through the trees. All those who were there wore red and black robes. They all began to dance with their torches and though they knew I was there, totally ignored me.

I did not recognize the music or understand the words, but these were from my small congregation. From behind, three men grabbed my arms and legs carrying me towards a wooden cage.

I struggled helplessly until they threw me in the cage. I looked in horror as they danced around the cage sticking torches through the openings. Two red robed individuals lit the trees on fire around me.

Smoke was everywhere as they sang and danced around the cage. I felt dizzy collapsing to the ground. The morning sun awoke me. As I looked around my woods were charred and my house was in rubble.

I noticed the cage was unlocked and quickly ran to my house. A sign was left on the only piece of wood left of my home. The sign read only one word: "Leave"

Play With Me

Cheryl and I finally found the house we wanted to live in. It already had a wooden fence surrounding the back yard which would keep prying eyes from disturbing us.

The family what lived on the other side decided not to welcome us, but we weren't into making friends. Usually it meant someone coming over to borrow something that would never be returned.

Cheryl told me she heard a little girl behind

the fence laughing and giggling. However, when she looked over the fence, no one was there. The laughing came again it seemed from a playground set near the house.

I was raking the next day and heard the little girl, too. A small volleyball bounced over the fence and the little girl's voice asking for it back. With a smile, I tossed it back over the fence.

"You're welcome" I said even though she didn't thank me.

"Who are you talking to?" Cheryl was at the back door.

"That little girl next door." I went back to raking leaves.

"Play with me." The ball came over the fence again.

"I'm working." I answered her gently.

"Please?" She seemed to beg.

I walked over to the fence and looked over without seeing her. I did hear her laugh around the corner of her house. I wasn't willing to play hide and seek so went back to raking. I saw the ball and threw it back into her yard.

"Play with me!" The little girl's voice sounded angry as the ball came back over the fence.

"Don't you have friends?" I asked her wondering why she was home alone.

A face appeared in the back window of the house with a quizzical look. I threw the ball back over the fence and was growing weary of this game.

"What are you doing?" The woman from

the window ventured outside to confront me.

"Your daughter needs a playmate." I tried not to sound annoyed.

"My daughter?" She looked confused.

"Yes, she keeps asking me to play with her." I lay my rake on the fence before facing her.

"My daughter died here two years ago." The woman's eyes swelled up with tears.

"Then who...?" I was at a loss for words.

"It wasn't my daughter." As she went back inside her house.

I Heard Death Say

I didn't expect to hear voices when I entered the hospital to see my wife. June was dying of cancer and it was sad to see someone so young turn into a human skeleton. The doctors had no hope, yet she was alert and in pain.

When I entered her room, she was talking out loud. I saw no one in the room and thought she was hallucinating. When she looked at me, I decided to ask her who she was talking to.

"Death." She smiled and stared right past

me.

"Death?" I was confused.

"I heard death say that he will be back to take me home." June seemed to relax relating this odd message.

"I think they are giving you too much medicine." I said under my breath.

"I know I'm dying, dear." June looked up at me with a sense of pity. "And it's all right."

"Not for me." I almost cried out.

We had been married for forty years and never left her side. I would even gladly change places with her if I could.

"Shall I leave you a list of those things you need to remember?" She started to laugh, but a coughing fit stopped her.

"Not funny." Though I was amused with her

sense of humor even now.

"He comes often to give me a sense of peace." June stared over at the other side of the room.

I followed her gaze and thought I saw a vague shadow sitting in the chair next to her. Now she has me seeing things. I felt a twinge in my chest forcing me to sit down on the other chair near the window.

I held June's hand for quite a while as she drifted off to sleep. The pan in my chest began to feel more acute. I wanted to call out for a nurse, but the words stuck in my throat.

The shadowy figure holding June's other hand began to become clearer. There was more substance so that I could almost see him clearly.

My eyes became heavier as my head fell to the side of the bed.

I felt June squeeze my hand before becoming limp. I raised my head for a second seeing the dark figure letting June's hand go.

"Let her go." I heard death say, for it certainly was death that sat there. I drifted into a deep sleep before waking up in an ICU unit. The doctors told me I had had a heart attack brought on by my wife's death.

When the nurse left me alone, I saw a dark shadow sitting by my side. Despite knowing who he was, I felt a sense of peace.

I Spy With My Little Eye

My son had a favorite game called I Spy. We walked through the forest near our house spotting various things to continue the game. However, this day was different.

"I spy with my little eye a small man in a green and red suit with a pointed hat on his head." He was so serious which made me laugh.

I acted like I saw the gnome he described, but only saw a patch of brush moving in the wind. I patted his head ns we continued on.

"I spy with my little eye something with one

eye carting a large club." I wondered where he saw pictures of these creatures.

A branch fell close to us where it seemed my son saw the ogre. Other branches fell towards an open field. The wind had picked up and I just thought the branches were dead bringing them to the ground.

"I spy with my little eye, scales and flames just ahead of us." My son looked terrified.

I picked him up as he cried in my arms. Part of the forest was already in flames as a lightning strike started another patch of trees to burn. Whether it was the dragon my son saw or the lightning strikes, we hurried back home.

My son ran to his room and hid under the covers refusing to come out. I tried to comfort him without success. The thunderstorm raged outside shaking trees and flinging debris everywhere.

I don't know why I stared out the bay window toward the forest, but there was movement that caught my eye. I was sure I saw a large creature staring at the house with a smaller little man next to him.

A pair of large yellow eyes glistened through the rain from the underbrush. Sparks and a flurry of smoke puffs blew away in the wind.

I rubbed my eyes to get a better look as the bay window began to fog up. I wiped away the moisture only to find just the forest and the sound of heavy rain.

I'm Not Supposed To Be Here

My nightmares are becoming more vivid with the worst so far last night. I found Sallie, my wife, shaking me awake as I struggled in a nightmare with huge giant leaning over me. I was sweating and breathing hard as the nightmare seemed so real.

I tried to talk it out with Sallie, but it didn't help. All day long I worried about going to sleep that same night. I stayed up until two AM hoping if exhausted I would sleep without dreams.

The nightmares continued for the next week so that Sallie had me sleep in the spare bedroom. Each night Sallie work me up hearing me struggle and shout against this giant enemy that tried to kill me.

Sallie insisted I see someone about the problem. I saw a psychologist which helped for a couple of nights. I started to relax again until I heard Sallie cry out.

When I came into her room, I found the giant standing over her. I hit him with a chair and it was then I realized it wasn't a dream. I thought I wasn't supposed to be here. This should have been a dream or nightmare.

Sallie ran into the living room and called the police. I slammed and locked the bedroom door until the police showed up. When they came and entered the bedroom with guns drawn. They found nothing and the room was neat and clean.

They warned us about making false calls to the police and then they left. Sallie was still shaking as I held her. We thought about leaving and finding somewhere else to live.

Now it seemed we both were hallucinating when we slept. It was difficult to relax after it became dark. We took turns sleeping, watching over each other to be safe.

Since we did that, the nightmares stopped for a while. We tried napping during the day and found it was more restful. We began to believe the giant was a figment of our imagination or maybe something we ate.

After a month, we decided to just try and sleep normally. That same night the nightmare of the giant came back. I saw the creature strangling Sallie, blood dripping down her and legs. I tried to wake myself up, but realized it wasn't a dream. I watched as he threw her aside like a rag doll before slowly turning towards me.

Left For Dead

I don't remember how I found myself lying in a ditch. My car was nowhere in sight and if I was with someone, there was no one here now. I felt the blood running down my face and my arm and leg had wounds or bite marks.

I tried getting up, but it was useless. The road nearby was empty as I heard a slow rumble of thunder. I used my shirt to soak up the blood and decided if I didn't find help I might bleed to death.

I saw a car coming down the road. I was able to stand up and try to wave it down, but instead the driver sped up past me. I limped further ahead hoping to find a house or see another car that would stop and help me.

I still could not remember how I got this way, but since my car was gone perhaps I was mugged. Flashes of an image of a dog attacking me shook me to the bone.

I tried harder to remember when I thought two men and a woman were standing over me. The woman had a cane and the two men were holding knives.

Whatever happened did so while I was in the road. I envisioned a gun in my hand, but unable to use it. Perhaps I was trying to defend myself though I clearly was the loser.

I willed myself further until I spied a diner on the right. I fainted and fell to the ground. When I awoke, I was inside the diner with two police officers staring down at me.

"Is he the one?" one of the officers asked a man I saw in vision.

"Yes" The woman I saw with the cane answered.

I could hear a dog growling just outside the door with two men holding it back. I tried to speak so that the officers would know I was the victim.

"What happened?" The other officer asked the woman.

"He was hitching a ride and he looked okay

to pick up." She began to relate clearly looking at me as if she was disappointed I was still alive.

"When we let him in the car, he pulled a gun." One of the men spoke up. "That's when Jessie, our dog, bit his arm. We struggled to get him out of the car until it got out of hand."

"You thought he was dead?" The officer standing over me said.

"We tossed him out of the car and took off." The woman sneered.

It came back to me that I was in the middle of a carjacking just to meet up with my friends in the next state. I passed out again only to wake up on the side of the road a few miles from the diner.

The Mist

My wife, Susan, was obsessed with our town's legend of a yearly mist that overwhelmed everything within three miles. I say it was a fog coming from the nearby lake, but the moisture seeped through every house it surrounded.

There were rumors and history of disappearances of those who dared to enter the mist alone. Susan insisted that there was something sinister inside the mist. Those who vanished without a trace were visitors in the town.

Most of us thought of it as a hoax to perpetuate the legend by a couple of locals. The legend, also, was said that if no one is taken, the town would be utterly destroyed.

It was October again for the time of the mist to appear. Residents would lock up their homes and draw the blinds and curtains. The streets would be abandoned until the mist or fog dissipated.

I could not persuade Susan to stay inside as she waited for the mist to thicken. She held a large flashlight anticipating whatever was outside. I refused to go with her since there could be someone or something to the legend. Either that or a group of locals who intend to keep their secret.

She called me a coward which hurt, so I felt compelled to go with her. I didn't think it would help, but I brought my shotgun just in case. We could hardly see two feet in front of ourselves when I heard someone laughing . I couldn't tell where it was coming from.

I tried to hold Susan's hand, but she wasn't with me. I called out, but there was no answer. My words bounced off the wall of mist. I felt soaked from the moisture that covered my clothes.

I readied my shotgun incase whatever took Susan would come for me. Fear gripped me as I was sure something happened to Susan. I saw a light dimly on the other side of the mist. It appeared to just hang in the air.

A distorted face glared at me behind the light and it wasn't Susan. Its eyes flashed red and its hands turned to talons reaching out to me. I raised my gun and fired into the mist. A horrible cry pierced the night forcing me to drop the gun and hold my ears.

The creature I saw lay dead just beyond the mist that now started to dissipate. When it completely disappeared, I found Susan dead on the ground.

Shadows

I first felt a chill on the back of my neck when I walked home from work. It was a creepy feeling like a finger was tickling my skin. The first time, I didn't see the shadows following me on either side of me.

I always saw Milt, the neighbor's dog, when I passed by. He would wag his tail and bounce up to lick my cheek. This evening, Milt was nowhere to be seen even when I called him.

I thought I saw a shadow flit over the lawn

even though the sun had set. I hurried home and locked the door as a strong chill seemed to grab my throat. When I got inside, the feeling and the shadow disappeared.

There was a nice warmth that embraced me as I settled in and started a shower. Half way through I heard a crash from the living room. I quickly dried off and threw on a robe. Entering the living room, I found the sofa overturned and a lamp on the floor.

The front door was open. No one was there to answer for the mess. The hall closet door quietly closed as I started toward the outside. I picked up my decorator cane to defend myself if anything happened to jump out.

My heart beat furiously as that same chill gripped my neck. I was sure I saw shadows flitting back and forth over my front yard. I realized that my cane would be useless against them.

I started to laugh at myself for being a coward. These were just hallucinations without form or substance. I closed my door and locked it tight. Just to be sure, I opened the closet door finding little but a few coats and shoes.

The next day, I came home a little quicker than normal. The corner of my eye caught sight of more shadows racing towards me. I was able to get inside safely.

I leaned against the door and thought it might help if I hid under my bed. It was then the lights went out. It was totally dark and I found I couldn't move.

The floor beneath creaked slightly as if someone was tiptoeing around the room. I couldn't see anything, but I knew there was something there. I tried to find my phone without success. I didn't know how the police could help me, but I wanted to try.

I stumbled around finding the stairs and crawled up to the top. I sighed a sigh of relief until out of the darkness someone called my name. I don't remember anything after that.

If I Could Remember

When I opened my eyes, I found blood all over my shirt and pants. I searched the deserted house finding nothing that gave evidence of a mass murder scene or reason for the amount of blood on me.

There was a knife and gun on the floor in the kitchen in which I hesitated to pick up. When I called out, no one answered. It didn't take long before I realized I was in my neighbor's home. In the distance I heard the police siren coming closer.

When I looked outside a small crowd had

gathered near three policemen outside my house. I hesitated going outside for the sheer fact that I was covered in blood. Did I kill my family? Would I be in jail for life for something I couldn't remember doing?

I started searching my mind about what had happened, but I only drew a blank. The police were scratching their heads as they spoke to each other.

I looked down on the ground and saw a trail of blood leading to my neighbor's house. No one else saw it yet. An ambulance screamed and dispersed the growing crowd outside my home. Moments later, two covered bodies were placed into the ambulance.

I almost called out knowing it had to be my wife and daughter. One of the officers stumbled out of my house and threw up on the ground. He was comforted by his comrades who didn't look any better.

I knew they would find me eventually, so I slowly stepped out onto the porch. With guns drawn, two officers confronted me. I was cuffed and led back to my house. Inside, I found my wife and daughter completely unharmed, but covered in blood as well.

The room was bloody and bits of flesh lay on the table and chairs. It was a horrible and confusing sight. I asked the officers what happened, but they couldn't explain it either. They said my wife and daughter wouldn't explain and they thought it was because they were shock.

My wife came over to me and hugged me, telling me everything was all right except the mess. I could smell on her breath that she had eaten something rank.

Finally, she explained that two men broke into our house. I tried to defend them and ended up being knocked out. There was a struggle and in a rage my wife and daughter tore them to pieces.

The police told me that the bodies were torn to shreds. How these two women could have done it was beyond belief. They asked me if we had a dog which we didn't.

I looked over at my wife and daughter who both wiped their mouths and hid their eyes not before I saw a flash of yellow and red. There was no explanation so the police left as we began to clean up the mess left behind.

Turn Around

I have been on the police force for fifteen years and it baffled me when I encountered a serial killing. Four people were murdered with their throats cut, but were still alive when I came on the grizzly scene.

Each of the four said before they died that they heard someone say "Turn around." before they were attacked. They could not describe the killer since they died in the next breath.

There were no witnesses at any of the

crime scenes. The victims were three men and one woman with nothing to connect them. After the second murder, I noticed the same man standing around watching us. I tried to find him in the crowd, but walking towards him, he disappeared.

There were no clues of who could be doing this. I was summoned a week later to an attack underneath Harper's Bridge. When I got there a small crowd had gathered. One woman then beckoned me to the victim who was struggling to breathe.

I asked if he saw who attacked him as his eyes widened in terror. He gasped that someone walked behind and said "Turn around." A hand covered his mouth and something was on his throat.

I searched the crowd finding the same man

from the other murder scenes. I immediately jumped up and chased him down the street. I could see he was younger than I was, but I gained on him until a brick wall that surrounded Walker's Park obscured his retreat.

When I got to the edge of the wall and looked around, he was gone. When I got back to the scene of the crime, an ambulance was taking the body away. Two officers had taken a few statements which were not helpful.

No one saw anything, but did here the man cry out. They all said they arrived seeing the victim gasping for breath. I described the attacker as best I could, but it wasn't enough. A search was made without success.

It had been a long day as I finally came home to a dark house. I walked up the stairs feeling a presence behind me. I reached for my gun just in case.

It was like a dark shadow that seemed to breathe on my neck. Then I heard the words "Turn around."

Dark Journey

When the sun went down, it became so dark I couldn't see a thing. I heard the owl in my back yard and even the sound of voices. No one seemed concerned about how pitch black the night became.

I found myself bumping into things like a tree trunk and tripping over roots on the ground. I should have seen the moon and the stars, but even they were seemingly obliterated from my sight.

Was I blind? I held my hand in front of my face without a trace of an outline. I felt around trying to find the front door of my house. I called out for my wife, Ellen, but she didn't answer. I did feel something smooth that appeared to cover my head. However it was so sheer I was unable to pull it off.

I started to panic until I found the front porch and was relieved to find the front door open. Someone's hand grabbed my arm which startled me. It had to be Ellen as I tried to call her name.

I found the couch and lay down as the hand that grabbed me was trembling. I tried to think of the last thing I could remember seeing. As the sun was setting, large square object fly past my head.

It was then night fell blinding me. Whatever

it was covered my head, eyes and ears, but not my mouth since I could breathe and speak. I knew I was talking, but unable to hear what I was saying.

Something or someone was pulling on the thing that covered my head. I felt a thick liquid drip down my face as I started to drift away. The thing around my head gripped harder, yet it partially gave way from my right ear.

I heard weeping and now a few voices in a panic. I asked what was wrong and reached up to my face. Two strong hands prevented me from touching the thing that attached itself to my head.

"How do we get it off him?" A man close to me to hold back the part of my ear that was exposed.

"What is it?" I asked while Ellen cried in the

background.

"I've never seen anything like it." Another man said before my ear was covered up and the silence became deafening.

Without warning or explanation, this thing released me and escaped through the front door as paramedics came in. They attended my wounds though both of them cringed at what they saw.

I asked for a mirror, but they hesitated to do so. Ellen, reluctantly, handed me a mirror. What I saw wasn't me. My nose was flat and instead of two eyes, I had only one in the middle of my forehead.

The thing that changed me was never found and I was lost to a life of hiding in the dark and alone.

Dead Of Night

I suffer from insomnia and often seemed to hallucinate. Usually it is in the dead of night. I see creatures and monsters that try to tear at my flesh and disfigure my face.

Without family, I mostly sit up and read while listening to the radio. Nothing interests me on the television networks. Even during the day I see these things behind trees or on the corners of houses.

I cannot close my eyes as the horrors creep close and are more lucid. I'm afraid that closing my eyes puts me into their realm where I am defenseless.

My cousin, Jeremy, whom I confided in, decided to come live with me for a couple of weeks. He saw firsthand the terrors, though not by sight, what I was going through. I explained the creatures that walked at night around my bed, but that I was fearful when I closed my eyes for any length of time.

After the first week, Jeremy heard noises from outside his room, but when he tried to investigate, nothing was there. Sometimes his closet door would swing open. He could only explain that what he saw were demonic eyes until he turned on the light.

I sympathized for him and suggested he might want to leave. He refused and took to putting chairs against the doorknobs of his room and closet.

My nightmares began to subside as my cousin's got worse. I could hear him crying in his room and throwing things which were only in his imagination. I tried to calm him down, but he saw me as one of the creatures that entered his room.

For the first time I was able to go outside and breathe the fresh air. Jeremy stood at his window pleading for help. I know it was cruel to ignore him, but I seemed to be finally free of years of terror.

I had no way to help him except maybe getting someone else to take his place. It would not be me. In fact I refused to enter the house again for fear of being infected again.

I called various professionals to see if they

could help, but after one visit they all decided nothing could be done. They all had a dread fear of death or, at least, terror being in the same room with Jeremy.

The last thing I remember before leaving for good was the anxious miserable look on Jeremy's face as I drove away.

The Last Sermon

The skies were filled with thunder and lightning as I entered my church. There were momentous events happening throughout the world. My country elected a socialist Marxist along with the Senate and the House of Representatives. The world was collapsing in financial, moral and spiritual ways that no one could foresee.

Riots and crimes were everywhere. Even going to church was considered a crime, but allowed to occur. My Pastor was the last of those who taught scripture trying to give everyone hope.

Singing was not allowed or communion or hugs or even handshaking for the fear of pandemic that embraced the world. Millions were dying and left in the streets.

In here, those of us who still keep our sanity, prayed and wept for the worst of what was happening. Children either left their parents or betrayed them to the authorities.

In the streets, those who believed they had the right to sexually abuse anyone attacked each other in broad daylight. The news media lauded the new freedom of anarchy though it led to the destruction of all moral laws and abject poverty except for those in power.

The media applauded the death of God using the name of Christ as a foul vision to explain that the destruction of anything decent was the greatest good for mankind.

What brought me here was the news of a nuclear attack at South Korea and a declared war between Russia and China. My country had become bankrupt and militarily weak. It was used as a means to quiet the protests against the government and shut down large gatherings in churches.

There were only a hundred worshippers in the pews as our Pastor stood behind the pulpit. As he spoke, we could hear the screaming and crying just outside the sanctuary. Our nation was the last bastion of hope and life. Now there was nowhere to escape the chaos.

We were told and sing "A Mighty Fortress Id Our God." As we sang I felt goose bumps rising as it inspired us not to hold back but sing loud. Sirens were heard in distance as the police were approaching the church.

Someone had informed the police that a service was being held. We continued to sing until all at once the sound of trumpets blocked out everything. We looked out the window to see ……

Police Report #325A

We were called to a report of an illegal assembly at Crossover Church of God. Someone called about a meeting of over one hundred individuals worshipping without masks during a major pandemic.

I was the first to enter the church finding only two men and a woman babbling in the pew about all their friends and family just amazingly disappearing in front of them. They were mumbling about being left behind.

Searching the whole church, my partner and I found it completely empty. There was no evidence that anyone else had been there. I did catch a word from the woman crying in the pew and that was Rapture.

When I was young I remembered being taught that fantasy. My partner and I questioned the three separately who all said that they were with others singing A Mighty Fortress when the sound of trumpets overwhelmed the sirens they heard outside the church.

Halfway through the song one of the men suddenly didn't hear anyone else singing. Looking around, he said almost everyone disappeared. The three of them started to shiver and shake before going into shock as they wept about being left behind.

My partner went to answer a call on our

radio as I tried to comfort them and try to understand what really happened. My partner told me to leave them and answer a call of a fatal accident happening nearby.

As we drove back into town, we saw numerous accidents of cars and trucks without drivers that crashed into store fronts and pedestrians. There were people running around in a panic. Abandoned cars sat empty and already we saw rioting.

A terrible noise overhead turned our eyes upward as a 747 flew above us and crashing into a high school gymnasium. My heart beat fast watching the chaos and I remembered a Bible story of the end times.

I didn't care then and I care less now as I felt a sense of loss with an urge to curse God for this mess. I did feel a sense of joy for being alive and those who seemed to vanish without a trace.

My partner and I agreed that we were the lucky ones as we stopped to survey the dead bodies lying in the street. We joined the grisly search for bodies amongst the wreckage. All we found were empty cars and trucks.

There were those who wandered aimlessly listening to radio reports that came from all over the world. Announcements said that we were the lucky ones as a new age had started. We were not left behind but moved forward.

The speaker asked everyone to be calm and there was talk of rebuilding. The Pandemic was the cause of this panic. We needed a renewed faith in mankind and listening to the voices of reason.

Over and over again we heard "We are in

this together, we will survive and trust your leaders to raise you up." I felt depressed as those hollow words di not comfort me. It seemed my soul was ripped from my body.

I decided to just do my duty and join those who were obviously suffering from this calamity. We were reassured that it was a onetime event brought on by the pandemic. We were told this was happening worldwide, but not to panic. We were assured that if we could hear his voice, then we were the lucky ones.

The Legend Of The Ibyx

Southern legends always fascinated me. Most of them had rational explanations. One of the few was the legend of the Ibyx. According to locals in Lennox just outside the dark thick woods.

No one has ever seen the Ibyx and lived to tell anyone about it. Naturally, I had to find out for myself. I traveled down with three of my friends and two local guides. Those in the town of Lennox begged us to reconsider going into the forest.

We ignored the warnings and went in setting up camp in a lonely spot. My guides were nervous, but we were paying them well. I was glad that they were staying close with us since I doubt we could find our way back to the van.

Linda, Gerald and James were excited as I was to see this creature. We had searched other legends without success. Our two guides Billy Jo and Andy anxiously checked our rifles and hunting knives in case we did encounter whatever this thing was.

I think having six of us made it safer to trudge on. We started down an overgrown path covered with branches and moss. We left our camp behind as Billy Jo scouted ahead disappearing into the heavy brush.

We heard a quick yelp which forced us to follow her. We found her body torn to shreds a short distance from us. Andy cursed before bringing us back to our camp. Andy hurried ahead of us.

I was a little more cautious with my friends. When we finally reached the camp, Andy was impaled on a tree above the camp that had been torn apart. A mournful howl came from behind the camp.

James and Linda panicked first while grabbing their rifles. They headed to the sound of what we thought was the Ibyx. I thought I heard laughing as Gerald and I checked our rifles.

Shots were fired which kept us away from the sound. I didn't want to get shot. None of us knew how to get out of the forest safely. I could only guess where the path was. I saw Gerald's eyes glaze over as he repeated: It was supposed to be like this."

We still heard James and Linda firing their guns, but I pulled Gerald away with me. I guessed the direction of the van. The gunfire stopped abruptly. I looked around coming toward only to hear the sound of grunting toward us.

I reached over to pull Gerald away with me, but he was gone. I was terrified that this thing would take me next. Running hard, I burst out into an open field where my van was parked. I clicked open the side door and jumped in.

I fell to the floor behind the driver's seat and waited. I saw an old blanket on the seat and covered myself. I heard the grunting just outside my window. The sun was setting, but I had no desire to see what the Ibyx looked like.

As the darkness filled the night, I listened to the grunting and the scraping of the paint on the van. I didn't sleep since the Ibyx circled my van and the sound of creaking metal.

In the morning as the sun rose, a certain stillness came about me. I allowed myself to uncover and peek outside. Nothing was there and I sighed a sigh of relief.

Soon the voices of hikers walking nearby stopped pointing at my van. I stepped outside seeing the twisted metal and splotches of blood on the hood. When the police came, I tried to explain what happened, but they only shook their heads in dismay.

Don't Blink

I know I have a vivid imagination, but lately, it has become dangerous. Images of leathery green creatures would appear and disappear every so often when I blinked too fast. It got worse when the wind blew dust in my eyes.

I tried to walk in the park thinking I might be safer. I was just inside the park when vision of that creature was seen reaching out to me with its long talons.

"You're suffering from the hallucinations,

too?" A man's voice looked concerned as he approached me.

"What are you talking about?" I asked seeing a rather tall man with a bushy beard stood in front of me. He had a tired look as if he hadn't slept in days.

"You look like you haven't slept in weeks." The man offered his hand. "Do you see a creature appear and disappear without warning?"

"How did you know that?" I asked hoping he had an answer for seeing this terror.

"I see it, too." The man shook his head.

"How long?" I wondered how it came to be with him.

"Since August sixth." He started to blink rapidly. "You?'

"September sixth." I wondered if the day had something to do with it.

"Mine are becoming more vivid where the creature's breath burned my skin." He rubbed his cheek absentmindedly.

"Is there no hope for us?" I asked thinking this man had an answer.

"Don't blink." In which he smiled sadly knowing it wasn't a joke.

"Today is August sixth." I reminded him. "It's been a year for you then?"

"I'm worried that I cannot keep my sanity for much longer." The man began to tremble.

"Are you all right?" I asked seeing his eyes were bloodshot.

"I feel..." The man started to cry as slight ripples undulated under his skin.

"Shall I call for help?" I wanted to help in some way.

"Too late." The man fell to the ground.

As I looked down, all I saw were a pile of clothes. The man had vanished. I wanted to run away myself, but where would I go. I started to blink rapidly seeing the creature now before me with talons dripping in blood.

My year would be up next month and I didn't see how I would escape the same fate. If I stayed out of the park would I keep from dying as well? All I could do is wait and see. Maybe if I could prolong blinking, I could gain some more time.

Ghost Garden

Jenn and I invited two other couples to visit the Ghost Garden just twenty miles from us. It was almost a theme park with, supposedly, five haunted houses. Actually, they were run down houses from the twenties which were long abandoned along a dead end street.

Two of the houses were advertised as places where ghosts were found of mass murderers that roamed the halls. The other three were said to be haunted by creatures like trolls, vampires and werewolves.

We were excited as Jenn and I went first to one of ghost houses. Our friends divided up to going into looking for creature in the other houses. John and Linda to the old Victorian and Sam and Susan to the crumbling two story on the opposite side of the street.

Jenn and I were disappointed at first since all we encountered was a sense of depression and a cold breeze now and again. The fact that the house was completely quiet unnerved both of us. Jenn had liked the air of foreboding until a shadow drifted by us down the hall.

I thought I heard someone say "Help me!" but it was so faint that I questioned if it were my imagination. We both agreed to go to the end of the hall and see what made the shadow. We both shook with anticipation hoping it was a real ghost.

Unfortunately, we found no evidence except that there were no footprints in the dust on the floor. I heard again the same "Help me!" but it was still faint as if coming from outside.

We found ourselves outside the back of the house were a mostly decaying garden greeted us. It was getting dark as we wandered past dead trees and drooping dying flowers. None of the garden had been watered in a long time.

There wasn't anyone watching the houses or even a guide to help us, we saw the shadow again sifting in and out of the cedar grove leading to the street.

I was determined to find out who it was. Jenny ran ahead of me thinking she could catch up to whoever it was. I followed her finding myself alone on the street in front of the old Victorian house.

I called out to her without an answer. I called again hearing answer "Here!" coming from inside. I wanted to see how John and Linda fared in their quests for monsters. I followed the sound of Jenn's voice finding myself a great hallway with a stairway covered in cobwebs.

I called out to John and Linda without a reply. Maybe they were exploring the rooms at the end of house. I called out to Jenn and only got silence as an answer.

The sound of a dog froze me in place. The snarling was close though I saw nothing. A heavy grunting came from the basement as something big and heavy labored up the basement stairs.

We were told of Trolls and werewolves living here and I was beginning to believe it, I had to find Jenn so I swallowed my fear and started toward what had to be the den. There I saw Linda lying on the couch with her throat bleeding. Her eyes were blank staring up at the ceiling.

Now I panicked since this was supposed to be a fun outing. I hurried toward the kitchen where, I thought I heard movement. On the kitchen table laid John with his clothes shredded and blood dripping down the table leg.

I thought I heard Jenn's voice from outside weeping about being lost. When I ran outside, her voice came from the old house where Sam and Susan went in. I cautiously entered finding the inside looking worse than the old Victorian.

I called out to Jenn with the sound of laughter echoing throughout the house. Breathing hard, feeling my skin crawl, I searched for Jenn before calling out for Sam and Susan. I found a staircase with a trail of blood leading upstairs. I hoped not to find any of them lying in a pool of blood.

"Help me!" the voice was louder now. I started to panic and couldn't decide what to do. I continued up the stairs following the trail of blood. It led to a small bedroom which I pushed the door open finding Susan hanging from a hook in the ceiling.

I turned to run as the bedroom door slowly closed in front of me with John impaled on the back. I howled in terror almost falling down the stairs. To my surprise Jenn was standing just outside in the street.

Then I heard the laughter from behind me as Sam and Susan came out of the house. Across the street, John and Linda appeared with what I thought was blood on them. The, too, laughed at my distress. I thought, very funny, the joke was over.

There was something wrong with them as their eyes looked empty staring blankly at me. I rubbed my eyes and when I opened them again, they were gone. I ended up calling the police who came by.

There was search as they found the bodies of all of them. Even Jenn was found lying in the ghost garden. The police were convinced I had killed them all. Nothing I said would convince them otherwise.

As they took me away, I looked up at the old Victorian seeing Jenn standing at the living room window staring in my direction.